THE STORY OF
A STUFFED ELEPHANT

LAURA LEE HOPE

THE STORY OF A STUFFED ELEPHANT

CHAPTER I

THE ELEPHANT AND THE MOUSE

"Oh, how large he is!"

"Isn't he? And such wonderfully strong legs!"

"See his trunk, too! Isn't it cute! And he is well stuffed! This is really one of the best toys that ever came into our shop, Geraldine; don't you think so?"

"Yes, Angelina. I must call father to come and look at him. He will make a lovely present for some boy or girl—I mean this Stuffed Elephant will make a lovely present, not our father!" and Miss Angelina Mugg smiled at her sister across the big packing box of Christmas toys they were opening in their father's store.

"Oh, no! Of course we wouldn't want father to be given away as a toy!" laughed Geraldine. "But this Stuffed Elephant—oh, I just love him!"

Miss Geraldine Mugg caught up the rather large toy animal and hugged it tightly in her arms.

"Be careful!" called her sister. "You may break him!"

"Oh, he's just a Stuffed Elephant!" laughed Geraldine. "I mean he hasn't any works inside him to wind up. He's just full of cotton! But I am beginning to like him more than I care for some of the toys that do wind up. I almost wish I were small again, so I could have this Elephant for myself!"

"He is nice," admitted Angelina.

"Well, I'm glad they like me," thought the Stuffed Elephant to himself, for just now he was not allowed to speak out loud or move around, as the Make Believe toys could do at certain times. But these times were when no eyes of boys, girls, men or women were looking.

It was mainly at night, after the store was closed for the day, that the toys had their fun—talking to one another, moving about, doing tricks, and the like of that. Now all that the Stuffed Elephant could do was to stand on his four sturdy legs, with his tail on one end, and his trunk, almost like a second tail, at the other end of his body.

He had two white tusks sticking out on either side of his trunk, and at first you might have thought these tusks were toothpicks. But they were not. An elephant's tusks are really teeth, grown extra long so he can dig up the roots of trees and the plants on which he feeds.

But a Stuffed Elephant doesn't dig with his tusks, of course. He never has to eat, being already stuffed, you know. And the Elephant in this story was well stuffed with cotton.

"I am sure this Elephant is going to be one of our very nicest Christmas toys," went on Miss Geraldine Mugg, as she lifted more playthings from the big box that had come from the workshop of Santa Claus at the North pole.

"Yes, I wish we had more like him," added Miss Angelina.

The two ladies helped their father, Mr. Horatio Mugg, in his toy store. It was a delightful place for children, and many a boy and girl would have been glad to stay all day in the "Mugg Toy Shop," as the big sign out in front named the place.

"Well, here are some more of those China Cats," went on Miss Geraldine, as she lifted some white pussies from the box.

"Oh, aren't they darling!" exclaimed her sister. "Do you remember the first China Cat we had?"

"Indeed I do! It was bought for a little girl named Jennie. And she told me, only the other day, that her China Cat had had ever so many adventures!"

"The dear child! The children, I believe, really think their toys are alive, and can move about!"

"Of course we can, only you don't know it, and you never see us!" whispered the Stuffed Elephant to himself.

And then he winked one eye at a China Cat—an eye that neither Angelina nor Geraldine saw blinking. Gracious! how surprised the two ladies would have been to see a Stuffed Elephant winking one eye at a China Cat.

But stranger things than that are going to happen, I promise you!

"Be careful, Geraldine! Be careful!" suddenly cried Angelina, as her sister arose from stooping over the box, and started toward the shelves with an armful of toys.

"What's the matter?"

"Why, you nearly stepped on the Stuffed Elephant!"

"Oh, I'm glad that it didn't really happen! We have only one toy like him, and it would never do to have him crushed all out of shape before he is sold for Christmas. I forgot that we left him standing on the floor. Gracious, but he's a big fellow!" she exclaimed.

"I'll lift him up on the shelf," Angelina said.

She picked up the Stuffed Elephant. Really he was one of the largest toys that had ever come from the workshop of Santa Claus. And he was a very finely made toy, only the best cotton and cloth having been used.

"Does he squeak?" asked Geraldine, as she saw her sister set the creature with trunk and tusks on a broad shelf.

"Squeak? Goodness, of course not! What made you think that?"

"Well, some of the toy animals have a squeaker inside them, and make a noise when you press it. I was thinking perhaps the elephant had a squeaker."

"No. If he had anything he would have a sort of trumpet in him," said Angelina. "Real elephants make a trumpeting noise through their trunks, but of course a stuffed one can't!"

"Oh, ho! You just wait until it gets dark and this toy shop is closed!" whispered the Stuffed Elephant to himself. "Then I'll show you whether I can trumpet or not. Though I forgot. I can't show you nor let you hear, it isn't allowed. But after the store is closed we'll have some fun!"

Toy after toy was taken from the big packing box. There were Sawdust Dolls, Candy Rabbits, Tin Soldiers, Plush Bears and a Monkey on a Stick—just like other toys of the same name who had had many adventures, and about whom stories like this have been written.

As the toys were taken out of the box they were placed on the shelves in Mr. Mugg's store. This was in a back room, for the toys had yet to be sorted and looked over, to make sure each one was all right, before they were put in the front part of the store to be sold.

Mr. Mugg had a larger and finer store than the one before the fire, when the China Cat had so nearly been melted by the great heat. And, having a larger store, Mr. Mugg bought larger Christmas playthings, such as the Stuffed Elephant.

Finally all the new toys were taken from the box and placed around on the shelves. While Angelina and Geraldine had been doing this, their father was in the front part of the store, waiting on customers. After a bit, when it grew dark outside, and the lights were lit inside the store, Mr. Mugg locked the front door and came back into the rear room.

"I think we have worked enough for to-day," the toy man told his daughters. "We will wait until to-morrow before looking over the new things and marking prices on them. I am tired and want to go to bed."

"Good!" thought the Stuffed Elephant. "That is, I'm not glad Mr. Mugg is tired," he went on, in his thoughts; "but I'm glad he is going to bed so I can move about and talk to some of my toy friends. It's been no fun to be shut up in that box ever since I came from the shop of Santa Claus."

A little later the store was in darkness, except for a small light burning near the safe, so the passing policeman could look and see that no burglars were breaking into it.

"Hello, everybody!" suddenly called the Stuffed Elephant, waving his trunk around in the air. "How are you all?"

"Who is that speaking?" asked a Nodding Donkey, a toy whose head kept moving all the while, as it was fastened on a pivot.

"A new chap—a Stuffed Elephant," answered a Jumping Jack, who wore a blue and yellow cap.

"A Stuffed Elephant! Let me see him! I never heard of such a creature!" brayed the Nodding Donkey, and he slid along the shelf to get a better view.

For it was the mystic hour when the Make Believe toys could pretend to be alive—when they could move about and talk.

"Here I am, right over here!" trumpeted the Stuffed Elephant, and if Miss Geraldine and Miss Angelina, or even Mr. Mugg, could have heard him they would have been very much surprised.

"Oh, you have two tails!" cried the Nodding Donkey.

"No, only one," said the Stuffed Elephant. "The other is my trunk. It really is a long nose, but it is called a trunk."

"Is there anything inside it?" asked a Calico Clown.

"Nothing but air—I breathe through my trunk," the Stuffed Elephant answered. "But I, myself, am filled with the very best cotton, lots and lots of it! Have you cotton inside you?" he asked the Donkey.

"No, I'm wood clear through," was the reply. "But as long as you are a new toy, let me welcome you among us. We are glad to see you. What is the latest news from the land of Santa Claus?"

"Well, let me see. So many things happen up there that I hardly know where to start to tell you about them," replied the Stuffed Elephant. "In the first place——"

"I'm stuffed, too!" suddenly interrupted a high, squeaky voice. "Only I'm stuffed with sawdust. Here I am, over here!"

"Yes, Miss Sawdust Doll, we see you," brayed the Nodding Donkey. "But please don't interrupt the Stuffed Elephant. He is going to tell us about Santa Claus, and I want to hear, as it is some time since I came from the North Pole."

"Well, I can tell you as well as that Stuffed Elephant can," went on the squeaky Sawdust Doll. "I came from Santa Claus's shop in the same box with him."

"You're not the first Sawdust Doll, though. She was bought by a little girl named Dorothy, I've heard said," remarked a rubber dog.

"Yes, that's right," said the Nodding Donkey. "And her brother Dick had a White Rocking Horse. But as long as the Stuffed Elephant kindly offered first to tell us the latest news from the North Pole, I think it would be only polite to let him finish."

"Oh, of course—yes!" squeaked the new Sawdust Doll.

"Well," began the creature with the trunk and tusks, "I think I will tell you——"

But just then there was a whirring noise at the end of the shelf, and a little voice cried:

"Oh, save me, somebody! Please save me! I'm wound up too tight, and my wheels are running away with me! I'll run to the edge of the shelf and fall off! Save me, somebody, please!"

A Rolling Mouse, that could run across the room on wheels when wound up, dashed along the toy shelf. As she had said, she was in danger of falling off. Straight toward the Stuffed Elephant ran the Rolling Mouse, squeaking in fright.

"I'll save you! I'll save you!" trumpeted the big toy. "Don't be afraid, Miss Mouse! I'll save you!"

He uncoiled his long nose of a trunk, and stretched it out toward the Rolling Mouse.

CHAPTER II

THE MAN AND THE ELEPHANT

"Catch me! Save me! Catch me before I fall off the shelf and break to pieces!" squeaked the Rolling Mouse.

"Don't be afraid! I'm right here!" trumpeted the Stuffed Elephant.

On his sturdy legs, big and round and stuffed with cotton, the Elephant stepped to the edge of the shelf. As quickly as the China Cat could blink her eyes, the Elephant reached across with the tip of his trunk and caught the Rolling Mouse just as she was going to slip over the edge of the shelf.

Holding her very gently, so as not to squeeze the breath out of the Mouse, the Elephant lifted the tiny creature up in the air, keeping her there until her spring ran down. Then, in a spirit of fun, he reached around and set the Mouse down on his broad back.

"There you are!" laughed the Stuffed Elephant in his hearty voice. "There you are, Miss Mouse!"

"Yes, but where am I? Oh, so high up as I am! Oh, where am I?" squeaked the little mouse.

"You're up on my back," laughed the jolly Elephant toy. "Don't be afraid. Stay there and I'll give you a ride to where you came from. On what shelf do you belong?"

"Oh, put me down! Oh, I'm so afraid I'll fall off!" cried the tiny mouse. "It is almost as high up here, on your back, as it would be to fall to the floor from the shelf. Do please put me down, kind Mr. Elephant!"

"Don't be silly, Miss Mouse!" brayed the Nodding Donkey. "The Elephant is good and strong, and he is also careful. He will not let you fall."

"Are you sure?" asked the little Mouse, trembling.

"Of course I will not let you fall!" chuckled the Elephant. "Just stay quietly on my back, and I'll take you where you came from."

"But maybe her wheels will go around again and make her roll off," remarked the Sawdust Doll.

"No, the spring unwound as I slid across the shelf," said the Rolling Mouse. "I'm all right now. Mr. Mugg wound me up to-day to show me to a little boy. But the boy wanted a pair of skates, and not a mouse like me. So Mr. Mugg put me down on the shelf without letting my spring unwind. He stuck me up against a Tin Soldier, and the Soldier kept me from rolling around. But just

8

now the Soldier came out to look at the new Stuffed Elephant. That left nothing to hold me back, and away I rolled."

"Oh, I'm sorry," said the Tin Soldier, touching his red cap in a salute to Miss Mouse.

"I'll forgive you, as I know you didn't mean to do it," said the Mouse toy, with a smile that made her whiskers wiggle. "But I do wish you'd put me down, Mr. Elephant. I am nervous up on your back, broad and big as it is."

"All right, Miss Rolling Mouse, I'll lift you down," trumpeted the Elephant. "And here you are at your own place on the shelf."

The big toy, stuffed as he was with cotton, reached back with his trunk, gently picked up the mouse in it, and set her down where she had started to roll from. As she had said, the wheels no longer whizzed around, as the spring which made them move had all uncoiled. It had "run down," as it is called.

"There you are!" went on the Elephant, after he had gently put down the Mouse toy. "Any time you are afraid of falling off the shelf, just call for me and I'll save you with my trunk."

"You are very kind," said the Mouse. "And so big and strong!"

"Isn't he big, though!" giggled the Sawdust Doll. "I wonder if he is strong enough to give me a ride on his back?"

"Of course he is!" brayed the Nodding Donkey.

"Do you want a ride on my back, Miss Sawdust Doll?" asked the good-natured Elephant. "All right! Up you go!"

With a swing of his trunk he set the Doll on his back as he had done with the Mouse. Then the Stuffed Elephant carefully walked around among the other toys, taking care not to step on any of them.

"I'm glad the Elephant has come to stay with us," whispered a little Celluloid Doll. "I'd love to ride on his back, but I don't like to ask him."

"I'll ask for you if you're too bashful to do it," said the Calico Clown, and he did.

"Why, of course I'll ride you, too, Miss Celluloid Doll," chuckled the Elephant. "I'll ride all of you in turn—that is all but the very largest toys. They might make my seams come open and the cotton stuffing puff out."

For the Elephant was made of gray cloth, you know, and he was sewed together, his tusks of wood being stuck in on either side of his trunk.

"I thought Elephants were always afraid of mice," said the Celluloid Doll, when she was having her ride.

"Pooh! Me afraid of a little mouse!" laughed the big Elephant. "I guess not! What made you think that?"

"It's in some of the story books," went on the tiny Celluloid Doll. "The story says real, live elephants are afraid of mice because they fear the tiny creatures will crawl up the nose holes in their trunks."

"That may be all right for real, live elephants," laughed the big, stuffed toy. "But I am only make-believe, you know, like the rest of you toys. The Rolling Mouse couldn't get up my nose."

"And if I could I wouldn't, because you have been so kind to me," squeaked the little mouse toy. "Next time I ride on your back I shall not be so afraid."

"Would you like to ride now, Miss Mouse?" asked the Elephant, as he set down with his trunk a Fuzzy Duck who had just been given a ride around the shelf.

"Oh, no, thank you; not now," answered the Mouse. "And I think it will soon be time for us to stop our make-believe fun. It will be morning in a little while, and you know we can't talk or laugh or do anything in daylight, when Mr. Mugg and his daughters or any customers are in the store."

"I hope the Elephant will have time to tell us a little of what has happened in North Pole Land since we came away," said a Rocking Horse, who had been in the toy store a long time.

"Yes, do tell us!" begged the other playthings.

"I will," said the Elephant.

So the Elephant, swaying on his four big legs, in the same way that real elephants do, told the latest news from the workshops of Santa Claus, whence he had lately come with the box of other toys.

"Is Santa Claus as jolly as ever?" asked a Tin Horse.

"Just as jolly!" replied the Elephant. "More so, if anything. His whiskers are a little longer, and his cheeks are a little redder, but that is all. I heard him tell some of his workmen, as they packed me in the box, that he hoped I'd like it down on Earth, among the boys and girls."

"You're sure to like it," said the Nodding Donkey. "A brother of mine used to be in this store, and he was given to a boy who took very good care of him."

"And a sister of yours is owned by a little girl named Dorothy," a Cloth Rabbit said to the Sawdust Doll. "She has lovely fun, your sister has."

"You'll very likely go to some boy. It seems to me you are too big a toy for a little girl," said the Calico Clown to the Stuffed Elephant.

"What will happen then?" the Elephant asked.

But just then Mr. Mugg came in to open the shop for the day, and the toys had to stop talking and pretend to be stiff and unable to move. They always had to be this way when any one looked at them.

"Well," said Mr. Mugg, as he and his daughters began dusting the toys, ready for the day's business, "Christmas is coming, and we shall soon be losing some of our toys."

"You mean people will come in to buy them," smiled Geraldine.

"Yes," her father answered.

"Well, I hope this lovely, big Stuffed Elephant goes to some one who will take good care of him," remarked Angelina, as she moved the big toy farther front on the shelf. "Oh, my!" she exclaimed. "His back is all dusty!"

"Dusty!" cried Geraldine. "Did you let him fall on the floor?"

"Indeed I did not! He hasn't been off this shelf or moved since he was taken out of the box last night."

"Then I wonder how this dust got on his back."

"I haven't the least idea," answered Angelina. "But I'll take it off with a brush." This she did.

Of course you know how the dust got on the Elephant's back. It came from the toys who rode him along the shelf. And, though neither of the Mugg sisters knew it, the Elephant had moved from his place on the shelf. He had walked all about it.

People began to come into the store to look about for Christmas. As Santa Claus is so busy nowadays he has to let some of the toy buying be done by the grown folks, and a number of them came in to see what their little boys and girls would like.

Among those who passed by the shelf on which the Stuffed Elephant stood, was a jolly-looking man, wearing a big fur coat, for the day was cold and it was snowing outside.

"Oh, ho!" exclaimed the man, as he saw the Stuffed Elephant. "This is just what my son Archie wants—an Elephant! I'll get this for him, as he wrote Santa Claus a letter saying he wanted a Stuffed Elephant more than anything else."

"This Elephant is just from the shop of Santa Claus," said Angelina Mugg, as she stepped up to wait on the man.

"Is he, indeed?"

"Yes, he was taken out of the box only last night. He is well made and strong, and he has heaps and heaps of cotton stuffing inside him. Even if he fell over on a little baby, this big Elephant would do no harm, as he is so soft."

"He is, indeed," said the man, feeling the toy. "I suppose he doesn't bite?" he added, looking at Miss Angelina and smiling.

"Oh, of course he doesn't bite!" laughed Miss Mugg. "Shall I have him sent to your house so your son Archie will get him for Christmas?"

"Thank you, it is so near Christmas that I think I had better take the Elephant with me," said Mr. Dunn. "I have my auto outside, and as it is a closed car the Elephant will not take cold."

"I'm glad of that," said Miss Angelina. Very often she used to make believe the toys were real, and alive, and could take cold, and become ill. Of course she did not know that the toys really could move about after dark, when no one saw them.

"Yes, I'll take the Elephant with me," went on Mr. Dunn. "I'll hide him away in the attic until Christmas, and then let Santa Claus give him to Archie. That boy of mine just loves animal toys!"

A little later the Stuffed Elephant was standing in among some other packages in the back of the auto. On the front seat Mr. Dunn was guiding the car through the storm, for it was now snowing hard.

"My! This reminds me of North Pole Land!" thought the Elephant, as he looked out of the windows of the car and saw the white flakes swirling about. "The ground is covered, too!"

It had been snowing some time before Mr. Dunn went to the toy store, and now he was having hard work to make his machine plow through the drifts on the way home.

"They took me away in such a hurry I had no time to say good-bye to any of my toy friends," thought the Elephant, as he snuggled down in the blanket in the rear of the auto. For elephants need to be kept warm, you know—that is, real ones, and this Stuffed Elephant made believe he was real.

"But of course I shouldn't have dared say anything while people were around," thought the toy. "I hope I see some of them again, for it wasn't very polite to come away as I did."

All at once, as the auto was rolling along quite fast, it came to a sudden stop, with a bump and a jerk.

"Hello! We're stuck!" cried the man. "I must see if I can break through the snowdrift."

He backed the car and started ahead again, with the motor going full speed.

Bang! the car struck the snowdrift. There was a crash of glass.

"Oh, dear!" whispered the Elephant to himself, for he went toppling, legs over head, out through a broken window of the car. Into a deep snowdrift stuck the poor Stuffed Elephant.

The Stuffed Elephant Stuck in a Snowdrift. The Stuffed Elephant Stuck in a Snowdrift.

The Story of a Stuffed Elephant.

"Oh, this is terrible!" sighed the toy. "Oh, I am freezing to death!"

CHAPTER III

UP IN THE ATTIC

Banging puffing, and grinding noises sounded all about the Stuffed Elephant. Around him swirled the white flakes of snow, but he could hardly see them, for part of his head, part of his trunk, and one eye were stuck in the drift.

Mr. Dunn's automobile had lurched to one side as Archie's father tried to send it through a big, white drift. And the noise was made by the motor, or engine, of the car, working its best to force the car ahead. The glass window of the automobile had broken as it tipped to one side, a piece of ice flying through.

And it was through the broken window that the Stuffed Elephant had been tossed, right out into a snowdrift!

"Oh, but it's so cold! So cold!" said the Elephant, shivering.

Of course it was cold up at the North Pole where Santa Claus has his workshop, and there was more snow and ice than near Archie's home. But up there the Elephant had been inside the warm shop, just as he had been kept in the warm toy store, and, until a few minutes ago, in the warm auto.

"Well, I guess I'll have to back up and go around another way," said Mr. Dunn, after a while. "I can't make my machine go through that snowdrift. No use trying! I'll upset if I do! Hello, one of the windows is broken, too! I'm sorry about that, but I can go on with a broken window, which I couldn't do if I had a broken wheel. And I guess the toys won't take cold. Yes, I must back up and go home by another road."

Starting the car slowly, Mr. Dunn backed it out of the drift. The front wheels and the radiator, where the water is, were covered with masses of white flakes, but aside from the broken window no damage had been done.

"I'd better hurry home, too," said Mr. Dunn, talking to himself, a way some jolly men have. "It's snowing worse, and I don't want to be kept out here all night. I want to get back with the Christmas presents. Archie will surely like that Stuffed Elephant."

And then, never thinking that the Elephant had been tossed out of the broken window into a bank of snow, Mr. Dunn started his car off on another road, leaving the poor Elephant stuck in the drift.

"Oh, this is dreadful! Terrible!" thought the Elephant. "I am freezing to death! Santa Claus wanted me to have adventures, but none like this, I'm sure! What shall I do?"

Since there were no real persons up in the attic—no boys or girls or grown folks—to spy around, the toys and other things in the dusty top of the house could do as they pleased. The toys could pretend to come to life, and even such a thing as a Spinning Wheel could whirl about and speak.

Thus when the Spinning Wheel had invited whoever wished to get on and have a Merry-Go-Round ride, and the harsh voice had called: "Make way! Here I come!" the Stuffed Elephant hardly knew what was going to happen.

Then, all at once, a big brown Rat—a real, live rat and not a toy—ran from a hole in the corner, and, with a squeal of delight, jumped up on the twirling Spinning Wheel.

"Here I go on the Merry-Go-Round! I ride this way every night!" squeaked the Rat to the Elephant and the other Christmas toys which Mr. Dunn had hidden in the attic until it was time for Santa Claus to come around.

"Do you, indeed?" asked the Elephant. "You must have lots of fun."

"I do," answered the Brown Rat. "But who are you?" and he stood up among the spokes of the Spinning Wheel and looked over toward the moonlight patch on the floor where stood the new toy.

"I am a Stuffed Elephant," was the answer. "And I have just had the most dreadful adventure! I was pitched out of the auto into a snow bank."

"I don't like snow!" squeaked the Rat. "It's too cold. But I am glad to see you, Mr. Elephant. Don't you want a ride on this Merry-Go-Round?"

"Thank you, I'm afraid I'm too big," answered the Elephant. "And I never before saw a Merry-Go-Round that spun this way, like a wheel. In Mr. Mugg's store, where I came from, there was a toy Merry-Go-Round, but it spun like a top."

"I'm not a regular Merry-Go-Round," said the Spinning Wheel. "I just make believe I'm one up here in the attic. Time was when I used to spin yarn for the grandmother of Mr. Dunn. But now all yarn is spun in factories by machinery, and spinning wheels are out of fashion. So I am up here in the dust, and it makes the time pass more quickly to pretend I am a Merry-Go-Round."

"Yes, and we Rats and Mice have good times!" cried the brown chap, as he wound his tail among the spokes of the wheel, to hold on tightly as he spun around and around.

"I believe I'd like a ride, too," said a Tin Soldier, which was another toy Mr. Dunn had brought home.

"All right! Climb up!" called out the Rat.

So the Tin Soldier, being able to pretend to come to life since no prying eyes saw him, got up on the Spinning Wheel and rode with the Rat. The Elephant wanted to have this fun, but he was too large to get on the wheel.

"Besides," he said, "something might happen to my trunk." He was very proud of his trunk and his tusks, was the Stuffed Elephant.

Several days passed, during which the toys had to remain hidden in the attic, waiting for Christmas. They did not mind it, however, as they were left to themselves and could have fun.

At last, however, Christmas eve came, and when the house was quiet and still, when Santa Claus was on his way flying over the chimneys with his sleigh and eight reindeer, the Stuffed Elephant and the other toys were carried down to the parlor and placed beneath the Christmas tree.

And when Christmas morning came Archie Dunn came racing downstairs, in his little pajamas, crying:

"Merry Christmas! Merry Christmas! What did Santa Claus leave for me?"

"Go and look," replied his mother.

When Archie saw all his toys, but especially the Stuffed Elephant, the little boy shouted and clapped his hands for joy and cried:

"Oh, what a lovely Christmas! Oh, I always wanted a Stuffed Elephant, and now I have it! Oh, what a fine, big Elephant you are!"

He threw his arms around the stuffed creature's neck and hugged him so hard that the cotton stuffing almost oozed out of the Elephant's ears.

"I hope he doesn't squeeze me any harder," thought the Elephant, though he dared not so much as give a trumpet sound, and as for saying anything or waving his trunk—that was not to be thought of!

For Archie was there, and his sister Elsie, and Mr. and Mrs. Dunn and the servants—a room full of people—and of course the Elephant had to remain quiet.

"Look at my new Dollie!" called Elsie to Archie, and it is a good thing the little boy had something else to look at, or he might have kept on squeezing the Elephant until he was out of shape.

"Yes, your Dollie is nice, but I like my Elephant better," said Archie.

"Elephants is for boys an' Dollies is for girls; isn't they, Daddy?" asked Elsie.

"I guess that's right," replied Mr. Dunn. "But get dressed now, children, and have breakfast. Then you may play with your toys."

Archie and Elsie were so excited over Christmas that they did not want to stop to dress, or even eat. But they managed to get some clothes on, eat a little, and then they started again to play with the many presents Santa Claus had brought them.

About ten o'clock Elsie, looking out of the window across the snow-covered yard, gave a squeal of delight and cried:

"Oh, here comes Mirabell, and she has her Lamb on Wheels! Oh, now we can have fun, and I can show her my new Doll!"

"Is anybody else coming?" asked Archie. "I want to show somebody my Stuffed Elephant."

Elsie looked again, before running to the door to welcome her little caller.

"Yes," went on Archie's sister, "I see Joe, and he has his Nodding Donkey!"

"That's good!" laughed Archie.

Into the house came Mirabell, who carried a Lamb on Wheels, which had been given her as a present some time before.

"Course this isn't for Christmas," said the little girl. "I didn't bring out my Christmas presents 'ceptin' this," and she showed on her finger a gold ring that Santa Claus had left.

"And I got a steam engine, only I couldn't bring it over," said Joe, who used to be lame but who was better now. "So I just brought my old Nodding Donkey," he added. "He was in the hospital once, as I was, and Mr. Mugg mended his broken leg."

At the mention of the name "Mr. Mugg" the Stuffed Elephant began to listen more carefully. If he had dared he would have flapped his big ears, but that was not allowed.

"I wonder," thought the Elephant, "if he means the same Mr. Mugg of the toy store where I came from? I wish the children would go out of the room a minute until I could speak to the Nodding Donkey and the Lamb on Wheels."

But the children were having too much fun to leave the room. Mirabell with her Lamb and Joe with his Donkey looked at the presents Santa Claus had brought for Elsie and Archie. Then there came a ring at the door bell, and in came a boy named Sidney, with a Calico Clown, and a girl named Dorothy with a Sawdust Doll. These toys were not new Christmas presents, for Dorothy and Sidney had brought only their old toys, since it was snowing again.

The Stuffed Elephant was getting excited. He had heard these other toys spoken of by his friends in Mr. Mugg's store, and wanted to talk to them. But while the children were in the room he dared not say a word.

At last, however, Mrs. Dunn invited the little callers out to the dining room to have some milk and cake, and out they rushed, leaving the toys in the middle of the floor.

"Ah, at last we are alone!" said the Elephant. "Please tell me, Mr. Nodding Donkey," he said, "were you ever in Mr. Mugg's store?"

"I came from there," was the answer.

"So did I!" joyfully exclaimed the Elephant.

"I don't remember seeing you there," the Nodding Donkey said, swaying his head up and down.

"I was one of the very newest toys," went on the Elephant. "I suppose you were there last year, or the one before."

"Yes," said the Donkey, "it was some time ago, and I have had many adventures. Tell me, did you ever have a broken leg?"

"Mercy, no!" exclaimed the Elephant.

"Well, I did. And Mr. Mugg mended it for me," went on the Donkey, proudly. "This Sawdust Doll here," he went on, "has also had many adventures. Tell him about them, Sawdust Doll."

"Oh, it would take too long," replied Dorothy's plaything. "But they are all in a book. And Dorothy's brother Dick has a White Rocking Horse, and his adventures are in a book, too."

"For that matter I have had a book written about me," said the Donkey.

"So have I!" declared the Calico Clown, jumping up and down. "It tells about my trousers catching fire."

"I wonder if I'll ever have a book written about me," sighed the Elephant.

"Perhaps," answered the Lamb on Wheels. "You are much larger than I, and there is a book about me. But let's have some fun, now that the children are out of the room."

"All right," agreed the Elephant. "This is like it used to be in Mr. Mugg's store after closing time. What shall we do?"

"I know what I should like to do," said the Calico Clown, as he looked at the big stuffed toy.

"What?" asked the Nodding Donkey.

"I should like to ride on the Elephant's back," went on the Clown. "All my life I have wanted a ride on an elephant's back, and I never yet had the chance."

"You shall have it now," replied the kind Elephant. "I'll come over and get you. Can you climb up? I'm pretty tall, you see."

"I'll stand on top of this toy trolley car," said the Clown.

One of Archie's presents was a toy trolley car, and by jumping up on this the Clown managed to reach the Elephant's back.

"Now hold on tightly, and you won't fall," said the Elephant. "If I had thought, I could have lifted you up in my trunk, as I did the Rolling Mouse. But I'll lift you down again. Sit tight now."

So the Clown sat tight, and the Elephant walked around the room with him, giving the gay fellow a fine ride. The Sawdust Doll was just making up her mind that she would be brave enough to get on the Elephant's back, when, all at once, the Nodding Donkey cried:

"Quick! Quiet every one! The children are coming back!"

"Oh, let me get off your back!" whispered the Clown to the Elephant. "They must never see me up here. It isn't allowed!"

But he was too late! Before he could slide off the Stuffed Elephant, Archie, Elsie and the other children came running into the room!

"Oh! Oh! Oh!" they cried, as they saw the Calico Clown on the back of the Stuffed Elephant.

CHAPTER V

IN THE BARN

Hearing the shouts of the children as they hurried back into the room where the Christmas tree stood, Archie's mother came to see what the matter was.

"Oh, Mother!" exclaimed Archie. "Look! The Clown is riding on my Elephant's back! Isn't he funny?"

"He looks very odd!" said Mrs. Dunn. "Who put him up there? Did you lift Sidney's Calico Clown to your Stuffed Elephant's back, Archie?"

"Oh, no, Mother!" Archie answered. "It wasn't I."

"Nor I," said Elsie.

"And I didn't, either," said the other children in turn.

"Well," said Mrs. Dunn, looking from one to the other, "of course the Clown couldn't have gotten up on the Elephant's back by himself, and of course the Elephant couldn't have lifted him there with his trunk. Though I know a live clown could jump on a live elephant's back, and a live elephant could lift a live clown up in his trunk. But these are only toys. They must be moved about."

"Well, I didn't put the Clown there," said Archie again.

"Nor I!" echoed the other children.

And while this talk was going on the Elephant, the Clown, and the other Christmas toys were very much worried lest their part in the fun be found out. Of course we know how the Clown got on the Elephant's back, but Mrs. Dunn did not, nor did the children. They didn't know that the toys had the power to make believe come to life when no one was watching them.

"If they had only stayed out of the room a little longer, I would have had a chance to slip down off the Elephant's back, and all would be well," thought the Calico Clown. "But, coming in so quickly, they caught me! I hope they never find out about our having fun when they are out of the room, or they'll never leave us toys alone."

"How do you s'pose that Clown got on my Elephant?" asked Archie of his mother, a little later.

"I think some of you children must have put him there, and forgotten about it," said Mrs. Dunn.

"No! No!" the children cried.

24

"Well, then Nip must have been playing with the Clown and just dropped him on the Elephant's back," said Mrs. Dunn. Nip was Archie's dog, a great big fellow, but very kind and good, and especially fond of children. He was called Nip because he used to playfully nip, or pretend to bite, cats. He never really bit them, though.

"But Nip isn't here to take the Clown up in his mouth and put him on my Elephant," Archie said.

"Oh, I guess your dog ran in here while you were out in the other room, eating the cake and drinking the milk," Mrs. Dunn said. "Then Nip ran out again, after dropping the Clown. Anyhow, we don't need to worry about it. Go on with your Christmas fun."

This the children did. And having seen the Clown on the Elephant, Dorothy wanted to have her Sawdust Doll ride in the same way. So the Clown was lifted off and the Doll was lifted on.

"Oh, I'm having my wish! I'm having my wish!" joyfully thought the Sawdust Doll to herself, as she was put on the Elephant's back, and Archie pulled the big, stuffed animal about the room.

The Elephant, too, was glad to give his friend the Doll a ride on his back as he had carried the Rolling Mouse and the other toys, though of course he could not speak and tell her so, for there were children in the room. The Doll, too, would have been glad to thank Mr. Elephant, but it was not allowed.

So all the Stuffed Elephant could do was to swing his cloth trunk to and fro, as Archie pulled him over the smooth floor, and all the Sawdust Doll could do was to wave her arms a little.

The children thought it such fun to give the smaller toys rides on the back of the big, Stuffed Elephant that they shouted and laughed with glee, making a great deal of noise. And there was more noise when Dick, who owned the White Rocking Horse, came over with his friend Herbert, who had a toy Monkey on a Stick.

"Oh, my dear children! You are making so much noise!" called Mrs. Dunn, entering the Christmas tree room. "Don't you want to go out in our big barn to play?"

"Isn't it cold out in the barn?" asked Mirabell, as she looked from the window and saw the snowflakes falling. "I wouldn't want my Lamb to catch cold."

"It isn't cold in our barn," Archie answered. "It has steam heat, 'cause my father doesn't want the horses to catch cold. And he doesn't want the water in our automobile to freeze, either, so he has steam heat in our barn."

"And it's warm and cozy," added Elsie. "Oh, out there we can have a lot of fun!"

"Let's go out there then," said Joe. "My Donkey likes it in barns, I guess."

"And so will my Elephant!" called Archie.

A little later the children were running over the snow to the big barn on Mr. Dunn's country estate. The gardener had shoveled a path through the snow from the house to the barn; so the children would not get their feet wet. Each child carried some toy, and Archie had all he could do to clasp the big elephant in his arms. For Archie was a small boy and the Elephant was one of the largest toys.

Once, on the way from the house to the barn, Archie, carrying the Elephant, stumbled and nearly fell.

"Oh!" cried the little boy, as he slipped along the snowy path. "Oh!"

The Elephant wanted to cry "Oh!" also, but he dared not. He felt shivery and frightened, though, as he saw the banks of snow on either side of him.

"I don't want to be pitched into another drift, head first," he thought to himself.

But Archie did not fall, and the Elephant did not get a second bath in the snow, for which he was very glad.

Into the warm barn trooped the children with their Christmas toys, some old and some new. Jake, the man who looked after the horses, giving them oats from a big bin, and hay from the loft, opened the doors for the children, and laughed to see how happy they were.

"We're going to play here and have a lot of fun, Jake!" called Archie. "See my big Elephant! I just got him for Christmas!"

"He is a fine fellow," Jake agreed. "Shall I put him in a stall as I do the horses?"

"No, we are going to keep him here to play with," said Archie. "And I think I'll get a little hay to make believe feed him."

"Well, be careful," warned Jake. "Don't fall off the haymow."

The haymow was a big place in the barn where the dried grass (which is what hay is, you know) was stored away. While the other children were having fun with their toys, Archie climbed to the mow to get some hay for his Elephant.

Now dried hay is slippery, as you know if you have ever tried to climb up a pile of it in a barn. And no sooner was Archie at the top of the mow than down he slid, on the hill of hay.

"Oh, I'm falling!" he cried, and his sister and the other children came running to see what would happen.

Archie slid down the haymow toward the floor of the barn. And it seemed as if he would get a hard bump. But, as it happened, a lot of the hay slid along with the little boy, and it was under him when he struck the barn floor. So he fell on the hay, which was like a cushion, and Archie wasn't hurt in the least. In fact he rather liked it.

"Oh, this is fun!" he cried. "I'm going to slide down the haymow some more!"

Again he climbed to the top, and down he slid, sitting upright as though on a chair. Again he slipped over the edge of the mow and fell on the pile of hay on the barn floor.

"Hurray!" shouted Joe, who, being no longer lame, could play like other boys. "I'm going to try that!"

He did, as did the other boys and girls, and soon they had forgotten their Christmas toys for the time being, in the newer fun of sliding down the hay. Thus the Elephant, the Donkey, and the different make-believe animals were left to themselves in a distant part of the barn.

"This is our chance," said the Donkey to the Elephant. "Let's walk around. My legs are stiff, especially the one that was broken and which Mr. Mugg mended."

"Yes, a little walk will do us good," agreed the Elephant. "I am a bit stiff myself, and I want to swing my trunk."

So the Donkey and Elephant, making believe come to life, walked about the barn floor, while the children were farther off, sliding down the haymow.

There were many strange things in the barn—at least strange to the Elephant and Donkey. There were garden tools of all sorts, rakes, hoes, shovels and picks. There were strange pieces of machinery for cutting hay, planting corn and potatoes, and the like.

In one corner was a big wheel, with a rope around it, and for a moment the Elephant thought his friend the Spinning Wheel had come out to the barn to play. But a second look showed that this wheel was larger, stronger and different in every way.

"I wonder what this wheel and rope are for?" said the Elephant to the Nodding Donkey.

"I don't know, I'm sure," brayed the nodding toy.

Just then the wheel turned slowly, and the long, dangling rope swayed to and fro.

"I wonder what that is for!" went on the Elephant. Like most animals he was curious about something he did not understand, just as your cat or dog will try to find out what causes a strange noise.

"Why don't you reach up with your trunk and feel it?" asked the Donkey. "I have heard you say your trunk was almost like a hand to you."

"It is," the Elephant answered. "I will feel the rope and wheel and see what it is like."

As the children were in another part of the barn, having fun in the haymow, and as there were no prying eyes to watch, the Elephant could do as he pleased. He raised his trunk and stretched it toward the dangling rope.

And then, all of a sudden, something happened. The rope turned and twisted like a snake, a loop of it wound around the Elephant's neck, and a moment later he felt himself being lifted off the barn floor in the hempen coils. Through the air, like the pendulum of a big clock, he swayed, and as the rope pulled tighter and tighter the poor Elephant cried:

"Oh, my dear friend Nodding Donkey! I am in a terrible state! The rope is so tight it is squeezing all the cotton stuffing out of me! Oh, what shall I do?"

CHAPTER VI

A DANGEROUS SLIDE

Anxious as the Nodding Donkey was to help his friend the Stuffed Elephant, nothing could be done. For the rope had suddenly been pulled up, taking the Elephant with it. And there he swung, dangling to and fro, the coil of the rope getting tighter and tighter around his neck, choking the poor toy.

"Oh, I know all the stuffing will be squeezed out of me! I just know it will!" sighed the Elephant. "Then I'll look like a balloon with all the air out of it! Oh dear!"

"Can't you get yourself loose?" asked the Donkey. "I wish I could climb up and help you, but I can't."

"And I'd help you, for I am a good climber, only I can't get off my stick. I'm fastened on tight just now," chattered Herbert's Monkey.

"Well, something will have to be done, if I am to be saved!" called the Elephant, of course not speaking loudly enough for the children, in another part of the barn, to hear.

Archie and his friends were still having fun sliding down the slippery hay, and they were making a great deal of noise. But you know how it is yourself. You often get tired of playing one game and want to go to another.

It was this way with Archie and his friends. They slid and slid and slid on the hay until they had had enough of it. Then Elsie said:

"Let's go back and get our playthings. I want to see my Christmas Dollie."

Back to where they had left the toys trooped the children, and Archie, who ran ahead, was just in time to see his Stuffed Elephant swaying on the rope that was choking him.

"Oh, look! Look at my Elephant!" cried Archie. "He's hung on a rope! Oh, he'll be killed! Oh, dear!"

"Run and grab him down! Pull him down!" shouted Joe.

Archie ran, but by this time the rope was pulled up still farther and the Elephant was so far above the barn floor that even Herbert, who was taller than Archie, could not reach the plaything.

"Oh, stop!" cried Archie. "Stop hurting my nice Elephant, Rope!"

Archie's voice was loud and clear. Suddenly the rope which had been winding up, around the big wheel, came to a stop, and a voice called:

"What's the matter down there? Are any of you children hurt?"

"Oh, that's Jake!" exclaimed Elsie. "It's our man Jake!"

"What's the trouble there, Archie?" Jake asked. He was somewhere in the loft of the barn.

"It's my Elephant!" Archie answered, trying to keep from crying. "My nice, Stuffed Christmas Elephant. He's hanging on a rope!"

"On a rope!" exclaimed Jake. "Do you mean this wheel rope that I use to hoist up bags of oats to the bin here? Is it that rope?"

"I don't know—but it's some rope!" Archie answered. "Can't you save my Elephant?"

"Of course I can!" called Jake. "Don't worry! Your Elephant isn't alive—choking with a rope can't hurt him!"

"Yes, it can, too!" insisted Archie. "It can choke all the stuffing out of him and make him flat like a pancake."

"Well, yes, that might happen," admitted Jake. "But I didn't know any of your toys were tangled in the hoisting rope, or I would not have pulled it. Wait a minute, now, and I'll turn the wheel the other way and let your Elephant down to you."

Slowly the big wheel turned in the other direction, and the end of the rope that was about the Elephant's neck dropped toward the barn floor. The Elephant, also, began slowly to come down.

"Thank goodness!" said the toy to himself. "I could not have stood being hanged much longer. I'm glad it's over!"

And it was over a moment later when Archie could reach up, take the loop of rope from around his plaything's neck and set the Elephant down on the barn floor.

"How did it happen?" asked Jake. He came down out of the loft, or place where he stored the bags of oats. The oats were hauled to the lower floor of the barn. There a rope was put about each bag and it was lifted to the upper floor where it was stored in a bin. The lifting rope went around a big wheel, acting like a dumbwaiter in some houses.

Jake had turned the wheel by pulling on a second rope upstairs in the barn, and as the wheel turned it wound up the longer rope. It was the end of this rope that had looped itself about the Elephant.

"How did it happen?" asked Jake again.

"I don't know," Archie replied. "I left my Elephant here when I went to slide down the hay. When I came back he was on the rope."

"Some of you children must have left the Elephant too near the end of the rope," said Jake. "When I wound it up the Elephant became tangled in a loop, and of course he was lifted up."

"Nope! We didn't any of us leave the Elephant near the rope; did we?" asked Archie of his little friends.

"Nope!" they all answered.

"Well, that's queer," said Jake. "That Elephant never got on the rope by himself, I'm sure."

But that is just what the Elephant did, as we know.

"Anyhow I'm glad he's all right now," said Archie, as he looked carefully at his new toy. "None of the stuffing came out."

But it might have, if the Elephant had been left hanging much longer on the rope.

Finding that everything was all right and that none of the children was in danger, Jake went back to the oat bin. There was a long chute, or slide, from the upper bin to a box on the first floor of the barn. And the oats came rushing down this slide when a door in the top bin was opened. This door could be opened by pulling a rope near the horse stalls, and sometimes Archie was allowed to pull the rope, open the door of the large grain bin, and let the oats slide down the chute to the smaller bin on the lower floor.

But this day Jake was putting a new supply of oats in the upper bin, and Archie was not allowed to play near it. The little boy and his friends soon began having more fun with their Christmas toys, giving the Clown and smaller dolls rides on the back of the Stuffed Elephant.

Thus Christmas passed, New Year's came, and the Elephant lived and was happy in Archie's home. The Elephant did not often think of Mr. Mugg and his daughters Geraldine and Angelina. He liked it much better, did the Elephant, in Archie's house than in the store. Of course the toy store was a jolly place, but no boys or girls were permitted to play with the toys. They were there for sale, and could only be played with after being bought and taken home.

So the Elephant was glad he belonged to Archie, who was a boy that took very good care of his playthings. Nearly every day Joe, Dick or Arnold would come over to see Archie, bringing their playthings, and in this way the Elephant met many friends whose adventures are related in the other books of this series.

And at night, when Archie and Elsie were in bed, of course the Elephant, and the other toys in the Dunn house, had their usual fun. They would make believe come to life and talk and play about in the nursery or in the closet—wherever they happened to be left at the close of the day.

It was still winter, though Archie and Elsie wished spring would come so they might play oftener out of doors. And one rainy day, when it was too cold and stormy to be out, Archie and Elsie went to the big, warm barn to have fun. Archie carried his Elephant and Elsie had her Doll.

"Let's go upstairs to the grain bins," suggested Elsie, when they had played about in the hay for a time.

"Maybe Jake will let us open the bin door from up there, and we can watch the oats slide down the chute," said Archie. "I like to watch the oats slide."

"So do I," Elsie admitted. The grain bin was so built that the door of the chute could be opened from above or below.

Up to the upper floor of the barn went the two children, with the Elephant and the Doll.

"Are you here, Jake?" called Archie, but there was no answer.

"I don't guess he's around," said Elsie.

"I don't guess so, either," replied Archie. "But I don't guess he'd care if I let down some oats. I looked in the lower bin and there's hardly any there. I'm going to let some down the chute."

"I'll watch you," offered Elsie, as she set her Doll on top of a big oat box.

The cover to the box was open. Archie liked this because he could see the smooth oats go down the wooden chute, or slide, like so much water.

"I'll let a lot of oats down," the little boy said to his sister. He placed his Elephant on the edge of the bin, near the Doll. Then Archie pulled on the handle that opened the door. It was hard work, for the oats pressed against the door. Elsie came to help him, and at last the children managed to get it open.

"There they go!" cried Archie, as the oats began to pour down the chute.

"Yes, and there goes your Elephant!" shouted Elsie. As she spoke, the stuffed toy fell into the oat bin, and, a moment later, the poor chap was sucked into the smooth chute, with the running grain, and the oats closed over his head. Lost to the sight of the children, the Stuffed Elephant was taking a dangerous slide.

CHAPTER VII

THE BIG DOG

Archie was so surprised at what happened that, for a moment, he could do nothing but stand and look at the stream of oats gliding down the wooden chute to the bin on the floor below.

"There goes your Elephant!" cried Elsie again. "He fell right into the oats, Archie!"

"Yes—yes—I—I see he did!" stammered the little boy.

"I'm glad my Doll didn't go, too!" went on Elsie. "I guess I'd better take her away 'fore she tumbles in."

Elsie reached over to take her toy from the side of the oat bin where the Christmas Doll had been put by her mistress. But Elsie's foot slipped on some hay on the floor, she tried to save herself from falling, her arm struck her Doll, and, a moment later, the Doll was sliding down the stream of smooth oats as the Elephant had done.

"Oh! Oh!" cried Archie. "Look at your Doll! She went down just like my Elephant!"

"Oh, dear! Oh, dear!" wailed Elsie. "Where has she gone?"

"Down into the oat bin on the first floor," explained Archie. "The oats go from this big bin to the little bin where Jake takes them out to give to the horses. Don't cry, Elsie. We'll get your Doll back."

Archie had almost been going to cry himself when he saw his Elephant being buried in the rushing stream of oats. But when he heard his sister's sobs he made up his mind to be brave and try to help her.

Archie was so excited that he still held up the sliding door of the oat bin, and the grains kept on sliding down the chute, carrying with them the Elephant and Doll, though now the toys were not in sight.

"Come on downstairs and get my Doll!" begged Elsie, tugging at her brother's hand. "Come on and get your Elephant and my Doll."

"Yes, we'd better do that," Archie agreed.

Then he saw that he was still holding open the little door in the oat bin, so that pecks and bushels of the grains were still sliding down the chute.

"I'd better close that, or the Elephant and the Doll will be buried away down under so many oats they'll never get out," said the little boy.

He let go the handle that they had pulled to raise the door, and it dropped shut, thus preventing any more oats from sliding down the chute. Then he took Elsie's hand and hurried toward the stairs that led to the lower floor of the barn.

Meanwhile, as you have guessed, the Elephant and the Doll were not having a very good time. At first, when the Elephant felt himself fall in with the sliding oats, he did not know what had happened.

"I wonder what sort of adventure this is!" thought the Elephant. "It's almost as bad as being pitched out into a snow drift, though I'm glad it isn't cold. These oats are very scratchy, though, and they make me want to sneeze. But where am I going?"

The Elephant did not know. All he could tell was that he was being hurried along in the dark with a lot of oats, for it was dark inside the grain chute.

Down, down, down went the Elephant, just as he had gone up, up, up on the rope.

"Where shall I land?" thought the Elephant.

A moment later he found out, for he was shot from the chute into the almost empty grain bin on the lower floor. Out of the chute tumbled the Elephant, and he was very glad to be in an open space once more.

"But it is almost as dark as it was before," he said. A little light came from the top of the bin which did not close tightly, but it was only a little light.

But the Elephant's troubles were not over. For no sooner had he been slid clear of the chute, landing on his feet, very luckily, than more oats poured out, for Archie was still holding open the door of the grain bin up above. So many oats came sliding down the chute that they rose all around the Elephant like rising water around a rock. The oats rose to his knees, to his stomach, where they tickled him a little, and then began to rise over his back.

"Oh!" he trumpeted, raising his trunk as high as he could. "I am going to be covered from sight in the oats!"

And then, when the oats almost covered his eyes, he had a glimpse of the Doll coming down the chute, in a shower of oats.

"Oh, you poor child!" called the Elephant.

"Yes, isn't this terrible!" exclaimed the Doll. "Oh, how are we ever going to get out?"

The Elephant tried to answer, but now the oats rose over his mouth and he could not speak. Only the top of his head and the tip of his trunk stuck out above the oats.

The Doll, having come down a little later, was not so deeply covered by the grains. She tried to stand up, to keep her head as far above the oats as she could, but it was hard work. Around and around she slipped, from side to side.

More and more oats poured down, for Archie still held open the door, and at last the poor Doll was covered from sight, as was the Elephant.

And it was now that Archie and Elsie came racing down the stairs. Archie called:

"Jake! Jake! Come here! Where are you? Oh, my Elephant is in the oat bin, and so is Elsie's Doll, and we've got to get 'em out!"

"What's that? Elsie in the oat bin?" cried Jake, who had just come back to the barn.

"No, not Elsie, but her Doll!" shouted Archie. "And so is my Stuffed Elephant."

"Well, that isn't so bad as if one of you children were in the bin," replied Jake. "I'll help you, though. Show me which bin."

Archie told what he had done, and when Jake opened the bin on the lower floor it was brim full and running over with oats.

"You surely let down enough grain," said Jake.

"How are you going to get my Doll?" Elsie asked.

"And my Elephant?" added Archie.

"Oh, I'll shovel them out," said Jake. "Don't be afraid. I'll get the Doll and the Elephant."

"Well, you'd better hurry, 'cause they may smother," Elsie said.

"I'll hurry," promised Jake.

With a shovel he carefully took some of the oats from the bin, so that first Elsie's Doll could be seen, and then the Elephant came into view.

"There you are!" said kind Jake, as he handed the toys back to the children.

"My, wasn't that a terrible time?" said the Doll to the Elephant that night, when they were left by themselves in a closet.

"I should say so!" agreed the Elephant. "I never want anything like that to happen again! I hope I have no more adventures!"

But he was to have more.

For a time, however, nothing very exciting happened. Archie played with his Elephant and Elsie with her Doll, and their boy and girl friends brought over their toys to have fun with. Often they amused themselves in the big, warm barn, though never again did Archie go near the grain bin.

Sometimes Nip, the big dog, would go to the barn to play with the children, and once, though not meaning to, the Elephant gave the dog a scare. It was this way.

Archie had set his elephant down on the barn floor, near a big box. Nip, the dog, coming suddenly around the corner of the box, did not know the Elephant was there until a draft of wind swayed the Elephant's trunk, making it wiggle to and fro.

"Oh, my! A snake! A snake!" cried Nip, who was afraid of the crawling creatures. "It's a big snake!"

"Nonsense! I'm not a snake," said the Elephant, who could speak, since Elsie and Archie were in another part of the barn.

"What was it that looked like a snake?" howled Nip.

"It was my trunk. The wind blew it," was the answer.

"Hum!" said Nip, who, now that he took a second look, saw that there was really no snake, and nothing to frighten him. "Hum! I believe you did that on purpose, just to scare me!"

"No, really I didn't!" said the Elephant.

"Yes, you did, too!" barked Nip. "And, just for that, I'm going to play a trick on you!"

"Please don't!" begged the Elephant.

"Yes, I will!" growled Nip, who was a little angry, and not as kind as he might have been. "I'm going to carry you away off!" he barked.

Then, before the Elephant could do anything to save himself, Nip, the big dog, caught the soft Stuffed Elephant up by his back and carried him into a dark and distant part of the barn.

CHAPTER VIII

AN ELEPHANT JUDGE

"Let me go! Oh, please put me down! Where are you taking me?" called the Stuffed Elephant to Nip, the big dog.

Nip did not answer. This was not because he could not speak the toy language or the language of Stuffed Elephants. But Nip held Archie's Christmas plaything in his mouth, and you know a dog can't even bark when he has anything in his mouth. He can only growl.

Now, Nip was not a bad dog. And though he was playing a trick on the Stuffed Elephant, still Nip was not cross enough to do any growling. So he just kept still, and trotted along the barn floor, carrying the Elephant.

Nip, being a big dog, had no trouble in carrying the Stuffed Elephant, though the toy was rather large. Stuffed with cotton, as the Elephant was, he was not very heavy, you see.

"Stop! Oh, please let me go! Where are you taking me?" asked the Elephant again.

But Nip answered never a word. All the dog had said at first was:

"I am going to carry you away off!"

And he seemed to be doing this.

Through the barn he trotted with the Stuffed Elephant in his mouth. The Elephant had never been in this part of the barn before. Archie and Elsie never came here to play. It was too dark, and rather dusty and dirty, with cobwebs hanging down from the walls and ceiling.

Down the stairs trotted Nip, still carrying the Elephant. The dog trotted over to a dim and dusty corner, dropped the Christmas toy upside down on the floor and then barked:

"There you are! Now let's see you find your way back! I'll teach you to scare me by making believe your trunk is a snake!"

"Oh, but I didn't do that! Really I didn't!" exclaimed the Elephant, as he scrambled to his feet. He could move about and talk now, because no human eyes were there to watch him. "It was all an accident," he went on. "The wind blew my trunk! I didn't wave it at you to scare you by making you think it was a snake. Really I didn't!"

"Yes, you did!" said Nip, and away he ran, soon being lost to sight in the darkness of this part of the barn.

For a little while the Stuffed Elephant stood there, swaying slowly to and fro, as real elephants do. He reached out with his trunk and gently touched the wooden walls. He could dimly see things all about him, but he did not know what they were.

"Oh, dear!" sighed the poor Stuffed Elephant. "I don't like this at all! I wonder what I had better do?"

He was trying to think, and wondering if he could walk up the stairs and find his way back to the place where Archie had left him before Nip carried him away, when, suddenly, the Stuffed Elephant heard voices talking.

"Maybe he could settle it," said one voice.

"Well, I'm willing to leave it to him if you are," said a second.

"Who is he, anyhow?" asked a third voice.

"Oh, he's some sort of animal," went on the first voice. "He isn't an angleworm, I know that much, but just what sort he is I don't know. But he looks smart, and maybe he can settle this dispute for us."

"I am a Stuffed Elephant, that's who I am," said Archie's pet, speaking for himself. "And who are you, if you please? I can't see any one, but I hear you talking. Who are you?"

"I am the Garden Shovel," answered the first voice; "and I claim to be the most useful tool in all the world. Without me there never would be any garden, and things would not grow."

"Nonsense!" exclaimed the second voice. "I am the Garden Rake, and I claim to be the most useful tool the gardener ever uses. Without me the ground would never be raked nice and smooth, so the seeds could be put in. I should get the prize for being the most useful."

"How foolishly you talk!" put in the third voice. "Every one knows that I am entitled to the prize. Talk about shoveling the ground, and raking the ground! What can you two do by yourselves, or together, for that matter, if the ground is hard? Answer me that. You must send for me, you know you must!"

"And who are you?" asked the Stuffed Elephant, for this tool had not yet named himself.

"I am the Pick," was the answer. "And with my sharp points the hardest ground can be made soft, so the Rake and the Shovel can work. I am the most useful tool of all."

"No, I am!" cried the Rake.

"Indeed you are not! I am!" exclaimed the Shovel.

"Well, there we are! Just where we started!" complained the Pick. "Why not leave it to this gentleman animal here. What did you say your name was?" he asked politely, and then Archie's toy saw the Pick, the Rake and the Shovel step out from a dark corner and stand in a row before him.

"I am the Stuffed Elephant," was the answer. "This is my first visit to this part of the barn. What is it you want me to do?"

"If this is your first visit you have never seen any of us before, have you?" asked the Shovel.

"Never before did I see any of you," the Elephant replied.

"Just the proper one for a Judge!" declared the Rake. "He will be honest and fair."

"I'm willing to have him if you two are," said the Pick.

"What's it all about?" asked the Elephant. "I don't understand. What is a Judge?"

"Some one who tells the right from the wrong," answered the Rake. "Listen, Mr. Stuffed Elephant! Get up on that box, for a Judge must be above every one else, and we will tell you what the trouble is."

The Elephant got up on a strong, empty onion crate, and stood there with the Shovel, the Rake and the Pick standing in a row in front of him.

"You must say 'Ahem!' and bang on the box, like a real Judge," said the Shovel.

"Ahem!" coughed the Elephant, as loudly as he could. Then he took up a piece of wood in the end of his trunk, and banged on the side of the onion crate.

"Now this is like a real court," said the Rake, "and we shall have our quarrel settled."

"Oh, have you three been quarreling?" asked the Elephant Judge.

"Well, not exactly; and the quarrel is not an angry one," replied the Shovel. "You see," he went on, "we three tools work in the garden. Or, rather, Jake, the man, uses us when he works. Now I claim I am the most useful of the three. Jake always takes me out when there is a bit of ground to be spaded up, or turned over, when he wants to make the garden in the spring. So I think, Mr. Judge Elephant, Your Honor, that I am entitled to the prize."

"Hum! Let me see now," said the Elephant, trying to look very wise. "I suppose I must listen to what the others have to say."

"Oh, yes, indeed!" exclaimed the Rake. "We must each state our case, as in a real court, and then you shall decide who is right. Now, for myself—Oh, by the way, had you quite finished?" he asked of the Shovel, politely.

"Yes," was the answer, "I think I said enough to have the Elephant Judge give me the prize. Go on, Mr. Rake."

"Well," said the Rake, smiling a little to show his teeth, "I claim to be more useful than the Shovel. It is true Jake uses him to turn the ground over. But before the ground can be turned Jake uses me to take away the dead leaves and sticks that are not wanted. And even after the Shovel is used to turn the ground over, no seeds can be planted, and the garden can not really be made, until I am used again to smooth things over. So I claim to be the most useful tool."

The Rake stepped back in line with the others, and they all waited for the Elephant to speak.

"Ahem!" said the animal judge very loudly. "There is one more to be heard. Proceed, Mr. Pick."

The Pick, who had at least two good points in his favor, stepped forward, made a stiff little bow with his handle, and said:

"What my friends Rake and Shovel have told you, of course is true. They are useful, each in his own way. But I do the really hard work of the garden. When the earth is packed hard and dry, so that neither the Shovel nor the Rake can be used, Jake always comes and gets me. I am larger and stronger than either the Rake or the Shovel, though of course the Rake has a longer handle. But it is a very thin handle, and if Jake struck as hard a blow with the Rake as he strikes with me, the Rake's handle would break. And no matter how hard he digs the Shovel into the hard ground, no earth can be turned over until I first loosen it. So I claim the prize."

The Pick stepped back in line with the other two, all three bowed politely and waited.

"What am I to do now?" asked the Elephant.

"You must act as Judge and tell which of us is the most useful, to decide who gets the prize," said the Rake.

"That is it," chimed in the Pick and the Shovel.

"This is very hard—very hard indeed," sighed the Elephant. "In fact I never before knew how hard it was to decide between right and wrong. Let me think a minute."

He passed his trunk over his head, which was beginning to ache with all the talk he had listened to.

"Hum! Let me see now," the Elephant spoke slowly. "It is true, Mr. Shovel, that you are very useful. Without you the ground could not be turned."

"There! See! I told you I'd get the prize!" cried the Shovel.

"Wait a minute! Wait a minute!" trumpeted the Elephant. "I have not finished. It is also true," he went on, "that the Rake is very useful. Before the Shovel can be used the ground must be raked clean, and after the Shovel has spaded the earth, it must be raked smooth."

"There! I knew it! Oh, what a fine Judge! He is going to say I am entitled to the prize!" exclaimed the Rake, laughing.

"Not yet! Wait a minute!" cried the Elephant. "I have not finished! I want to say that the Pick used very good arguments. He is right when he says without him, in case the ground is hard, nothing can be done. And he certainly is the strongest, so I think——"

"Oh, ho! What did I tell you! I get the prize!" cried the Pick.

"Wait a minute! I have not finished!" said the Elephant Judge. "What I was going to say was that before I could decide who wins I must see the prize. What is the prize? Bring it here that I may see it, and then I will decide who is to get it."

"Wait a Minute!" Trumpeted the Elephant. "Wait a Minute!" Trumpeted the Elephant.

The Story of a Stuffed Elephant.

"Oh, the prize!" cried the Shovel.

"That's so, we forgot all about it!" gasped the Rake.

"What was the prize to be?" asked the Pick. "I declare we did not settle on any. How stupid!"

"Until I see the prize I cannot give judgment," said the Elephant; "so the case will have to 'go over,' as I believe they say in Court, until the prize is brought here. Stop disputing now, and get me the prize!"

"Yes! Yes! The prize! The prize!" cried the Rake, the Shovel and the Pick, and away they scurried.

"Ha! Ha! Ha!" laughed another voice in the corner whence had come the three tools.

"What silly chaps!" came in another voice.

"To forget the most important thing of all—the prize!" added another.

"Who are you, if you please?" asked the Elephant, stepping down off the onion crate.

"I'm the Hoe," was the answer of the first. "If I had wished I could have told how useful I am. In fact, I think I will have a try for the prize."

"I'm just as much entitled to it as you are," some one else said. "You needn't think you can get ahead of me!"

"Who are you?" asked the Elephant.

"The Wheelbarrow," was the reply. "You ought to see the loads I carry. I ought to get the prize!"

"What about me?" asked a third voice.

"Who are you?" asked the Elephant.

"The Lawn Mower. Just think what an ugly place this estate would be unless I kept the grass trim and neat. It should be my prize."

"Oh, my goodness!" exclaimed the poor Elephant. "If there are to be more disputes, and more evidence in this case, I shall go mad. Stop!" he cried, as the Wheelbarrow, the Hoe, and the Lawn Mower came forward, all talking at once. "Stop! I will do nothing until I see the prize! Court is adjourned!"

And as the Elephant said this the sound of loud barking sounded through the barn.

"Oh, maybe that is Nip coming to carry me back," thought the Elephant. "I certainly hope so!"

CHAPTER IX

OUT IN THE RAIN

You remember that Nip, the big dog, had carried away the Stuffed Elephant when Archie set his Christmas toy down on the barn floor for a moment. And, coming back, after having gone to look for the nest of a cackling hen, Archie did not find his Elephant awaiting him as he expected to.

"Oh, Elsie!" exclaimed the little boy. "Didn't I leave my Elephant right here?" and he pointed to the place where he had set it.

"Why, yes, I think you did," Elsie answered. "I saw you put it there. I was going to leave my Doll there, too, but she isn't feeling very well, and has a little cold, so I carried her in my arms. I have her here now," she added, as she held up her Christmas toy.

"Well, my Elephant is gone!" exclaimed Archie. "And I know I left it here! Yes, you can see where his feet stood," he added, as he pointed to some marks in the dust of the barn floor.

Elsie, holding her Doll, stooped down beside her brother and looked at the dust.

"There are lots of marks," said the little girl. "Your Elephant must have been walking around. Oh, Archie!" she cried, with shining eyes, "maybe he came to life and walked away!"

"Nope! He couldn't do that!" Archie said. Of course he knew nothing of what the toys did after dark—how they made believe come to life, talked, and had fun among themselves.

"But now I know what has happened!" Archie exclaimed. "I can tell by the marks in the dust."

"What did happen?" asked Elsie.

"Nip has been here," went on the little boy. "I can tell his paw marks in the dust. It wasn't my Elephant walking around, it was Nip! And Nip has carried off my Elephant!"

"Oh, just as he did once with my old Rag Doll!" cried Elsie.

"That's it!" her brother said. "Nip has carried away my Elephant. Come here, Nip! Where are you?" called Archie.

Now Nip was always ready to come when Archie called, for he and the little boy had many good times together, romping and playing tag in the yard. So, when he heard his name called, Nip came running into the barn to where Elsie and Archie were standing.

"Nip!" sternly said Archie, as he shook his finger at his big dog, "did you take my Elephant? Did you carry him away?"

Now Nip understood a great deal that was said to him. He knew when he was being scolded for having done wrong, and he knew he was being scolded now. He also knew that he had taken away the Elephant. So, when Archie talked this way, Nip hung his head and put his tail between his legs.

"Nip!" went on Archie, "where is my Stuffed Elephant? Go get it! Bring back my Elephant! Go on, Nip!"

Nip gave a little bark. He sprang up, barked again, louder than before, and off he ran to a dim and distant part of the barn.

"Is he going after your Elephant?" asked Elsie.

"I hope so," her brother answered. "We'll follow him and see where he goes."

But Nip ran too fast for the children to follow. Down the stairs, into the dark corner of that part of the barn where the garden tools were kept, ran Nip. He knew he had been found out, and that he must bring back Archie's Elephant.

So, just as the Shovel, the Rake and the Pick had hurried away to look for the prize, and while the Wheelbarrow, the Hoe and the Lawn Mower were fussing to see why they couldn't have a chance to win, Nip pounced down on the Elephant, lifted him up, and started back with him to Archie.

"Oh, I'm so glad you came to get me!" said the Elephant. "I was just going to try to find my way back myself, for I have had a most dreadful time trying to settle a dispute among the garden tools. Oh, I never should like to be a Judge!"

Nip did not answer, because he had the Stuffed Elephant in his mouth.

"I hope we are going to be friends, Mr. Nip," went on the Elephant. "Please don't carry me away again."

Nip wanted to say that he would not, for he felt sorry because of the trick he had played. But just then Elsie and Archie came running up, and the dog could not talk, nor could the Elephant pretend to be alive, for the eyes of the children were upon them.

"Oh, he has my Elephant!" joyfully cried Archie. "I guess you must have hidden him, Nip, for you knew where to find him! Bring my Elephant here!"

Nip put the Elephant down on the barn floor at Archie's feet, and then the dog wagged his tail.

"He's asking you to forgive him," said Elsie.

"And I will," promised Archie. "But don't do it again!" he added, shaking his finger at Nip.

"Bow wow!" barked the dog, and perhaps that meant he would not.

"Oh, I'm so glad to have my Elephant back!" said Archie, as he began playing with his toy.

"And I'm glad to be back," thought the Elephant. "That Judge business was a great trial!"

Through the spring and into the summer Archie had fun with his Christmas Elephant. Then one day something very exciting happened. Archie was playing out in the back yard, near a little brook, with his Elephant, when along the front road came a hand-organ man and a monkey. Archie and his sister ran to hear the music and see the monkey, and Archie left his Elephant in the grass.

Soon after this it began to rain very hard and the children hurried into the house. Going up the steps Archie fell and bumped his head, making his nose bleed, and there was so much excitement for a time that the Elephant was forgotten. He was left out in the storm, and the rain came down harder and harder, making little puddles and tiny brooks in the yard; brooks that flowed into the large one.

"Oh, this is dreadful!" thought the poor Elephant, as the rain pelted down on him. "Of course if I was real I wouldn't mind the rain, for real Elephants like water. But I'm getting soaking wet! It's beginning to come through my stuffing. I'm feeling like a sponge!

"Oh, why doesn't Archie come and get me, or at least give me an umbrella! I think I'll try to walk under a toadstool to keep out of the wet. If I can only find one large enough."

As no one was watching him, the Elephant had a chance to move about and make believe come to life. But he had waited too long. The rain had soaked into his cotton stuffing making him so heavy that now he could not move.

"Oh, what is going to happen?" he thought.

He tried to lift first one leg, then another, but it was hard work. The water was beginning to rise about him. His feet were in mud puddles. He struggled hard to pull them out, and then, all at once, he lurched to one side, and fell over flat—right into a pool of water!

CHAPTER X

A VOYAGE HOME

Down pelted more and more rain, harder and harder, until the back yard, where Archie had been playing with the Stuffed Elephant, was almost a little lake of water. The puddle rose higher and higher around the Stuffed Elephant as he lay on his side, unable to move because he was so soaked with water—like a sponge.

Inside the house where Archie lived there was trouble, because the little boy was hurt worse in his fall than was at first supposed. They had to send for the doctor, and of course no one thought of the poor Elephant.

"I'm glad I'm not out in this rain with my Doll," said Elsie, as she sat at the window after the doctor had gone.

"Yes, it is a regular flood," said Mother, sadly thinking of her little boy.

And still no one thought of the Elephant out in all the storm.

If Elsie remembered anything at all, she probably thought that Archie had brought his Elephant into the house. As for Archie, the doctor had given him something to make him sleep, and the little boy was too ill even to dream of his Christmas toy.

As for the Elephant; well, he was in a sad state! The wet cotton stuffing inside him was cold and clammy. His trunk was like a wet piece of paper, and he feared his wooden tusks would come out, if the glue that held them in got too much soaked.

"Oh, dear! What am I to do?" thought the poor toy.

Now it happened that Jeff, the colored boy who had once taken the China Cat from Mr. Mugg's store after a fire, lived not far from Archie's home. Jeff and his folks had moved to the country from the city. And about this time Jeff's mother sent him to the store.

"Has Ah done gotta go in all dis rain?" asked the little colored boy.

"Yo' suah has, Honey!" replied his mother. "Yo' isn't salt or sugah, an' yo' won't melt. Put on yo' ole coat an' go to de sto'!"

So Jeff went. He took a "short cut" which led across the Dunn's back yard, and Jeff passed the place where the poor Elephant lay in a puddle of water.

"Oh, golly!" cried Jeff, his white teeth glistening against his funny black face as he laughed. "Ah'd done gone an' found annuder playtoy! Only dis one Ah done found in de rain, but de udder one was in a fiah! Ah knows whut Ah's gwine to do. I'll put dis Leffelant on a board till Ah comes back from de sto'. Den Ah'll take him home wif me!"

Jeff looked around until he found a flat board, large enough to hold the elephant. Putting the toy on this board, Jeff laid it to one side, and ran on to the store. He did not want to take the Elephant with him for fear some one would see it and ask him about it.

But Jeff was not to have that Elephant. While the colored boy was at the store the rain came down harder than ever, making so much water that the little brook in Archie's back yard rose higher and higher.

So high did the brook rise that the water reached the board on which the limp and soaking Elephant was lying on his side. And then the water lifted up the board, Elephant and all, and floated them down stream.

"Oh, my!" thought the poor Stuffed Elephant. "This is the last of me! I am going on a long voyage! I shall never see Archie again!"

Down the stream he floated on the board which was like a boat. Once a fish poked his head out of the water and called:

"Who are you and where are you going?"

Before the Elephant could answer the swift current had carried him farther downstream and away from the fish.

Once the board with the Elephant on it bumped against a big Water Rat.

"Be careful who you're bumping!" snarled the Rat.

"Be Careful Who You're Bumping!" Snarled the Rat. "Be Careful Who You're Bumping!" Snarled the Rat.

The Story of a Stuffed Elephant.

"Excuse me," replied the Elephant. "I didn't mean to."

The Rat tried to bite the Elephant's trunk, but again the swift current carried the boat downstream.

Finally the rain stopped, after a day or so, but by that time the Elephant had been carried a long way down the brook, at last coming to a stop when the board was caught in the roots of an overhanging tree. By now the Elephant was almost glued fast to the board, so wet and soaking was he.

The rain stopped, the brook went down, the sun came out, and the Elephant dried. But he still lay on the board, on the bank of the stream, under the roots of the tree.

A man, who happened to be passing, saw the Elephant, picked him off the board, and, seeing that he was an expensive toy, took the plaything to his home.

"What a fine Elephant!" said the man's wife. "I'll put him on the mantel, over the stove, so he'll dry out more. Some child lost this. We haven't any children small enough to want to keep it. I wish I could find out who owned this Elephant."

"I wish so, myself," thought the Elephant. "Oh, shall I ever get back to Archie?"

It was a day or so after the big storm that Archie was able to be up and around, and the first thing he thought of, when he could go outdoors, was his Elephant.

"Oh, where is he?" cried the little boy. "I 'member I left him in the yard when we heard the hand-organ music and ran to see the monkey. And then it rained and I fell down and bumped my nose. Oh, where is my Elephant?"

"If you left him out here in the yard I fear the Elephant has floated away," said Mrs. Dunn. "The brook rose very high—almost up to our back steps— and it probably carried your Elephant away."

"Oh, shall I ever get him back?" cried Archie, feeling sad.

"I'm afraid not," his mother answered.

Archie felt so bad about his toy that his father put an advertisement in the paper, asking whoever found the Elephant to please bring him back and get a reward.

If Jeff, the colored boy, had been able to read, he might have seen the advertisement and have told what he did with the toy.

But Jeff never read the papers. And, besides, it rained so hard when the colored boy went back from the store, after putting the Elephant on the board, that Jeff had to go home another way, and he forgot all about the stuffed plaything he had set aside.

But the man who had taken the Elephant home read the paper, and he saw the advertisement Mr. Dunn put in.

"There!" called the man to his wife. "Now I know where that Elephant belongs. I'll take him back to the little boy."

"Well, he's good and dry," said his wife. "I mean the Elephant is good and dry. He's almost as good as new." And, in fact, the Elephant was, for she had brushed off all the mud, and the heat had dried out the water.

Carrying the Stuffed Elephant, the man who had found the toy took it to Archie's house.

"Oh, here he is! My Christmas Elephant! He's come back to me! Oh, how glad I am!" cried Archie, as he clasped the cotton creature in his arms. "Oh, how glad I am!"

"And I'm glad, too!" thought the Elephant. "I feared I would never see Archie and Elsie again! And I'm even glad to see Nip!" for the dog came to the door, wagging his tail.

And so, after several adventures, the Stuffed Elephant was back home again, but many more things happened to him, though I have no room for them in this book. The Elephant even acted again as Judge in the dispute of the Rake, the Shovel and the Pick, but who won the prize I cannot tell. I think each should have had a prize. Don't you?

Once again there was happiness in the Dunn house, for the lost Elephant was back, and Elsie gave her brother a pink ribbon to tie on his toy's neck.

"It may look pretty, but it tickles me," thought the Elephant, as Archie pulled him about.

THE END